CROW

CROW

NICOLA SKINNER

ILLUSTRATED BY
REBECCA BAGLEY

Barrington Stoke

First published in 2023 in Great Britain by
Barrington Stoke Ltd
18 Walker Street, Edinburgh, EH3 7LP

www.barringtonstoke.co.uk

Text © 2023 Nicola Skinner
Illustrations © 2023 Rebecca Bagley

The moral right of Nicola Skinner and Rebecca Bagley to be
identified as the author and illustrator of this work has been
asserted in accordance with the Copyright, Designs
and Patents Act, 1988

A CIP catalogue record for this book is available
from the British Library upon request

ISBN: 978-1-80090-219-0

Printed in Great Britain by Charlesworth Press

For my mother, Christiane Skinner.

She read stories, found stories, wrote stories, and even sang stories for me, throughout my childhood and now.

Thank you, Mum.

CONTENTS

1. THE MOVE   1

2. MAKING FACES AND NOT MAKING FRIENDS   7

3. THE DEN   15

4. YOU'VE SQUISHED IT!   18

5. THE IDEA   25

6. THE PLAN   29

7. A FIGHT   38

8. THE STORM   43

9. ALIVE   46

10. BOOOOO   52

11. NOT A BAD IDEA   59

12. GETTING MORE FRIGHTENING   67

13. THINGS HAVE TO CHANGE   72

14. THE FIELD   81

CHAPTER 1

THE MOVE

We'd been in the van for three hours when my stomach began to churn. And it wasn't just the yukky sandwich I'd eaten at the motorway cafe.

I was worried. We were moving house. We were swapping the city of Bristol for a village in Somerset. We might as well have been moving to the moon – that was how little I knew about our new home.

I was starting at a brand-new school too. Every time I thought about that, the insides of my tummy swam and squirmed as if they were tadpoles.

At the new school, there'd be loads of children and teachers I'd never met. What if no one liked the things I liked? What if no one liked the way I talked? What if no one liked *me*?

I looked out of the van window. I felt so sick. How was I, Hattie Mole, ever going to walk into a classroom of twenty-nine children I'd never met before? What was I going to say? My tummy flipped over again.

As if he knew what I was thinking, Dad said, "Are you excited about your first day at school, love? What are you going to say when you meet your new class?"

"I could ask if anyone likes rats," I said slowly. "Then I'll tell them about my pet rat Sid and how amazing he is. I'll tell them that I have a brother too – that's you, Oliver – even if you're not as amazing as Sid. And I can tell them about you, Dad, even if you are messing up our lives for ever ..."

From the back of the van, Sid squeaked. *He* agreed with me. *He* understood how I felt.

"You can't say your rat is better than your big brother, Hattie," said Oliver.

"And is it fair to say I'm messing up your life for ever?" said Dad.

"But you *are*," I grunted. "I didn't ask to move house."

Dad turned the van into a narrow country road. I could smell cow poo. I felt even more sick but Dad actually opened the van window some more.

"Ah, the smell of the countryside," he said with a cheerful grin.

Dad hadn't been so happy for years! Things had been really hard for him. First, the restaurant he worked at closed, then he was looking for work but couldn't find any, then he got this new head-chef job he really wanted but had to find somewhere new for us to live.

He hadn't laughed for ages but now he was grinning away as if someone was tickling him.

"Look, I know you didn't want to move, Hattie. Just give things a go, all right? I think you'll be really happy at your new school. But maybe don't start off talking about rats – some people don't like them."

I huffed and puffed. What if rats didn't like humans either?

Oliver said, "Dad's right. Why don't you talk about how much you love making things? That would be a good way to make friends."

"No," I said. Because that stuff is private. It matters so much to me, I don't often talk about it.

"Just say you're excited to meet everyone then?" Oliver went on.

"That's a lie," I grunted.

Oliver went back to reading his book.

*

At last Dad stopped driving. We'd arrived at a village green with a duck pond. A sign said "WELCOME TO THE VILLAGE OF LITTLE PLUG".

A few ducks in the duck pond quacked at us as we got out.

In front of us was a small pink cottage.

"That's Sweet Pea Cottage. Our new home," said Dad.

CHAPTER 2

MAKING FACES AND NOT MAKING FRIENDS

We spent the weekend unpacking millions of boxes. Then on Monday morning, after Oliver had gone off to his secondary school on the bus, Dad and I walked to my new school together.

I was too nervous to talk, so I just tugged at my horrible new scratchy jumper. I hated how it felt and I kept trying to get it away from my skin.

"You're going to be fine," Dad said softly as he gave my hand a squeeze.

Walking towards us was a girl with green eyes and black hair. "Hello, I'm Katya," she said. "You're in my class. The teacher sent me to fetch you."

I bit my lips as I said goodbye and walked away from Dad. I didn't want him to see how nervous I was.

The walk to my new classroom went on for ever. I couldn't think of one thing to say to Katya. She seemed to know and just gave me shy looks as she played with a pretty bracelet around her wrist. She was still twisting it around when we got to a door that said "Mrs Simmonds' Class".

We walked inside. The room was hot and full of faces that I didn't know. The teacher gave me a big smile. "Hello, Hattie," she said. "I'm Mrs Simmonds. Welcome to Little Plug Primary."

Then everyone else said hello. It was very loud.

I smiled but I couldn't say anything. My mouth was dry and my lips got caught on my teeth, so I must have looked like an angry dog snarling at everyone.

My normal voice had vanished. I sounded like my rat, Sid, squeaking. Everything I'd thought about saying in the van had been scrubbed right out of my head.

It felt very quiet. I knew I had to say something.

"I have a rat," I blurted out. "And I make things and don't like talking about it, so don't ask. My brother is all right. My dad messed up my whole life."

There was a long silence that went on for what felt like a million years. Then my teacher told me to sit down, next to Katya. *At least things can't get any worse*, I thought.

I was wrong.

*

If you want to know what someone's really like, watch them eat. That's what Dad's always told us, and he's a chef, so he knows.

At lunch-time, the boy next to me ate his jacket potato so fast that he burned his mouth. Then he gulped down some water and he dribbled most of it down his school shirt. Yuk.

The girl on the other side ate her yoghurt first. Then a tangerine. She ate her cheese sandwich last. What sort of person starts with pudding and ends with a main? Another yuk.

Struan, a boy with red hair, talked with his mouth full and spat crumbs all over the table. Yuk number three. He chatted a lot to Katya.

Katya ate everything in the right order and didn't make a mess. But she also had clever green eyes that looked everywhere as if she could see everyone's secrets.

I miss my old school, I thought. *Everyone is new and strange here.*

I fiddled with the food on my plate – I was thinking too much to eat. Then it went very quiet. Everyone at my table had stopped talking. They were all looking at *me*. I'd been so busy watching everyone, I hadn't seen they were watching me *back*.

"What's *that*?" asked Struan, pointing at my plate.

I looked down and blushed. I'd made one of my food faces.

I'd started making food faces when I was small. When Dad took us into work, he'd sit us at a table near the kitchen, where he could watch us.

"Make me something," he'd say, and hand us some raw vegetables and crackers. It was his way of keeping us busy so he could do his work. Oliver and I moved the food around to make faces.

And now, on my plate for everyone to see, was a new food face. It had raisins for eyes and a carrot stick for a mouth, all stuck on a slice of bread to make a face.

Struan said: "Aren't you going to eat your lunch?"

I wanted to tell them that I wasn't hungry. That my tummy was tied up in tight knots. But I didn't know what to say because everyone was looking at me.

"I can't eat," I murmured. "This food face looks alive to me. Like a little bread friend."

"What's a bread-end?" asked Katya.

"Bread FRIEND. It looks ALIVE." I was shouting a bit.

No one said anything. We were all feeling bad.

"Shall we go and play?" said Katya.

Did she want to play with me? I wasn't sure. *Probably not*, I thought. I was too weird.

I looked away from Katya and down at my feet. I felt shy. Katya waited for a second, then she pushed her chair back and walked away. The others went with her. Lunch-time was over. I was no good at making friends.

CHAPTER 3

THE DEN

I didn't know how to get out into the playground. Instead, I went out the wrong way and ended up around the back of the school next to an old shed. There was some rubbish stacked up against it.

I heard children playing, so I followed the sounds and ended up in the right place at last. It had started to rain.

All the other children were busy and didn't see me. I felt very lonely and sad, so I had to squeeze my eyes tight to stop crying. *Being the new girl is horrible*, I thought.

Then I opened my eyes and saw something amazing.

It was at the end of the playground, set apart. A tree. Suddenly the day felt better.

Thick branches grew from the trunk of the tree. They went up, down and sideways, as if the tree had tried to grow every way it could.

I knew it was an oak tree, but really it was more like a house. The branches grew so that the tree was as wide as it was tall.

One of them curved up and down like a doorway. I checked to see if anyone was looking, then I stepped through the doorway under the branches and right up to the tree trunk. I took off my horrible itchy jumper and dropped it on the ground.

I closed my eyes and took a deep breath. For the first time that day, I felt OK. The smell of earth and leaves and rain made me feel calm.

This is the perfect den, I thought.

The leaves whispered around me. The sounds of the other children playing weren't so loud any more. For the first time that day, I didn't feel lonely.

I want this tree all to myself, I thought.

CHAPTER 4

YOU'VE SQUISHED IT!

The next day I ran over to the den at break-time. It was empty again.

If I can keep this tree all to myself, I thought, *I'll be OK at Little Plug Primary School.*

I took off my itchy jumper again and left it on the ground. And then I started to make things.

I picked up some old leaves from the ground. I stuck dandelion flowers into them, then tied them to branches with long grass.

Now I was making things, everything felt better. My mind went still as my hands got working.

I scooped up some damp mud from the ground. I patted the mud until it turned into a friendly looking egg shape. *What can I turn you into?* I thought.

There were some small brown leaves nearby. I picked them up and stuck their stalks into the mud ball until the mud ball had lots and lots of bristles all over.

The mud egg had turned into a small ... hedgehog. A mud hedgehog.

"Hello," I whispered with a grin. I made a few more because it felt so good.

Three little mud hedgehogs stood in a row on the ground and I was getting started on another one when I saw some black shoes standing just outside my den.

I looked up. They were Katya's shoes, and next I saw her green eyes and Struan's brown ones.

Katya looked at the hedgehogs and whistled. "More faces," she said, grinning. It was too dark in the den to see if she was being friendly or laughing at me.

Struan said, "Are you going to let us in?"

Katya said, "This is the school tree. Everyone needs to share."

"It's my den," I said, scowling at her.

"Well, aren't you a Baron of Laughs," Struan said.

"You mean *barrel of laughs*, Struan," said Katya, and then she looked at me with a big grin on her face. For a moment, I nearly grinned too. Perhaps she *was* being friendly? Maybe I could share the den.

Struan went a bit pink. "Doesn't matter," he said. "Let us in, Hattie?"

"Look out for the—" Before I could say anything else, Struan stepped right on top of one of my hedgehogs.

SPLAT.

He didn't even notice.

Had he done it on purpose?

It felt as if the den began to shrink around us. Struan was just walking around with half a mud hedgehog on his shoe.

"Ooooh, pretty," murmured Katya. She was looking at the leaves with the dandelions stuck into them. "Did you make these too?" she asked. She reached her hand out towards one of them. "How did—"

"Don't touch them," I said. "Or they'll probably get destroyed TOO."

I reached out to pull her arm away from the leaf. I didn't mean to hurt her but she gasped. "Ouch," she said. "Why did you do that?" She rubbed her wrist and twisted her pretty bracelet.

"Me? Err, hello? YOU STARTED IT," I shouted. "Struan squished my hedgehog."

"What hedgehog?" stammered Struan.

I pointed at the floor. "That one."

"That's a mudcake," he said.

"It is *now*," I wailed. "Because you killed it."

Then things got even worse. Three tiny Reception children ran in. One of them trod on my second hedgehog.

SQUISH.

Everyone at this school wanted to destroy my den. I hated them all.

"Hattie," said Katya quickly. "Listen." She looked like she was about to say something but I'd had enough.

I gave one last loving look around the den. Then I ran off and stayed away from the tree – and everyone else – for the rest of the day.

CHAPTER 5

THE IDEA

"How was your second day?" asked Dad when he came to pick me up from school.

I didn't know how to tell him. Instead, I said, "My school jumper is too scratchy and I hate it."

Dad looked at me for a second. Then he took my hand and squeezed it. "Let's walk home," he said. "I found a nice way back over a field."

At my old school, our walk home went through a supermarket car park. Sometimes for a treat we'd buy a packet of fizzy sweets and then stand and eat them on the flyover that went over the motorway.

Everything was different now. There was no flyover. Just a boring old footpath through a boring old field.

In the middle of it, far away from us, stood a shabby, lonely man with his arms stuck out. He had a faded red waistcoat. His head was on one side as if he was watching us.

"Dad," I said, trying to see the lonely man better. "Is that person all right?"

Dad smiled. "That's not a person. It's a scarecrow."

We walked a bit closer. I'd never seen a scarecrow before. I wasn't even sure what they did. The scarecrow was made out of old clothes and hay and old wood.

A crow landed nearby, looked up at the scarecrow and flew away with a loud squawk.

"Good job, scarecrow," laughed Dad.

I watched the bird fly off.

"Doesn't the scarecrow have to do anything?" I asked. "It just stands there?"

"Yes. If it's big enough, and scary enough, it will frighten birds away from the crops the farmer wants to protect. Like a guard. That's its job."

"Do you have to buy a scarecrow?" I asked.

"Oh no," said Dad. "Anyone can make a scarecrow."

Now that I could do.

That was when I got the idea.

I was going to make my own scarecrow. But not to scare birds away from a field. It would scare children away from my den. It was a brilliant idea and one that could not go wrong.

CHAPTER 6

THE PLAN

Back home, I went straight to my room and opened Sid's cage. As he ran up my arm, making squeaking noises, I began to think. I began to plan. I'd asked Dad on the way home how people made scarecrows and made a list in my head of all the things I'd need.

Dad was busy making dinner for us. *Perfect*.

I put Sid down and went into Dad's bedroom and found some of the stuff I needed for my scarecrow plan.

*

When you have to sneak what you need to make a scarecrow into school, everything has to happen at the right time.

The next morning, I went into Dad's bedroom very early and shook him awake. Parents who have just woken up don't know what's going on and you can make them do whatever you want.

I said, "Oh, Dad, I forgot. You need to drop me off early today."

"Wurg?"

"Why? Oh, because my class has an early – um – thing."

"Early thing?"

"Yes. Didn't you get the text message from the school? You need to take me there now."

Dad stared at me, trying to understand what I'd said.

I pointed at his alarm clock. "And I need to be there in five minutes. If I'm late, then you'll get a *letter from the school*."

Dad jumped out of bed. He hated letters from the school. "Yikes," he said.

My plan had worked.

He threw some clothes on and muttered that he couldn't find his favourite jeans. I went to get the bags that I'd packed up carefully the night before.

In the hallway, dressed and stressed, Dad took one look at my bags and opened his mouth.

I said, "They're for an art project. What's the time?"

Classic distraction move. He forgot all about the bags and drove me to school as we were in such a rush.

The playground was empty. "You have to press the buzzer," I said.

Dad pressed the buzzer. The gates opened. This was going better than I'd hoped. "Don't wait," I said. "It's embarrassing."

Once Dad was back in his car, I skirted around the back of the school to the shed I'd found on my first day when I got lost.

It was still there. *Great*.

And there were the old fence post and wooden broom I'd seen too.

I grabbed them and ran to the den. I had about half an hour before anyone else turned up, so I had to work fast.

I tipped the bags out onto the ground and looked at the items I'd collected:

1. Dad's favourite pair of jeans, ripped at the knees .

2. An old pink T-shirt, also from Dad

3. Some bits of newspaper

4. One of my pillows with a rainbow pattern

5. An old glittery baseball cap I'd borrowed from Oliver's room

Is this a stupid idea? I thought as I looked at everything lying on the ground in a mess.

"Hattie Mole, you make things all the time," I said to myself sternly. "And you can definitely make a scarecrow."

I set to work.

I stuffed one leg of Dad's jeans with newspaper until it was plump and full. I slid the fence post down the other leg, then filled that with newspaper too. Then I got the old broom. I picked up the hammer and nails I'd taken from the garage that morning and nailed the broom handle to the middle of the fence post.

It worked. The fence post and the broom handle met in the middle in a T-shape – the shape of a person with their arms out.

I put the pink T-shirt around the broom-handle arms and made sure both ends went through the sleeves. I stuffed the T-shirt with the last of the newspaper.

I still needed more stuffing, so I grabbed lots of damp leaves from the ground and filled the scarecrow up with those. They made the T-shirt wet and muddy but the scarecrow was getting fat and starting to look like a person.

There was only one thing left to do. I made a small hole in the pillow with a sharp stick. Then I pushed the pillow onto the top of the fence post.

I drew a face on the pillow with a black Sharpie pen I found in the kitchen. Two big black eyes, two fierce eyebrows, one grumpy mouth. Scary. Perfect.

The last thing was Oliver's glittery baseball cap. I placed it carefully on top of the head.

I dragged my scarecrow to the entrance of the den. I lifted him as high as I could and then pushed his fence post right down into the mud to fix him in place.

I wobbled him a little to check how steady he was. Not bad at all.

I stepped back and looked up into his face. "I need you to protect this den," I whispered.

The scarecrow looked back at me as if he understood.

He needed a name.

I whispered, "I'll call you Crow."

Then I turned away and left Crow to protect my den. I felt better already.

Crow would stop people from kicking things over. Crow would show Katya and Struan and all the rest of them that the den belonged to me.

From now on, I thought, *I can walk on my own to my den every break-time. All the other children will stay away and leave me alone. My scarecrow will frighten them off.*

CHAPTER 7

A FIGHT

But that wasn't what happened.

At break-time, the playground was full of the sound of laughter and no one left me alone.

Joe, the boy who ate too fast, had taken Crow out of the ground and was whizzing him around and dancing with him. Crow's pillow face was wobbling on his fence-post neck. His baseball cap lay on the ground.

All around Crow were children laughing and asking to have a turn next. Crow's eyes looked big and shiny.

I shouted, "Get your hands off him. He's not meant to dance. I made him to guard the den."

"What den?" asked Joe, looking puzzled.

Katya stopped laughing and turned to me. "I should have guessed," she said softly. "*You* made this."

"It's funny," added Struan. "Well done."

"It's not meant to be *funny*," I said.

I didn't tell them that he was wearing my dad's clothes and Oliver's old baseball cap. That he was made of bits and pieces of my family. I didn't tell them that I missed my old school, or that I felt weird around new people, or that my school jumper was scratchy, or ...

I just said, "Put him BACK."

Katya looked over at me. "You care more about this daft scarecrow than about making friends with us," she said.

"Yeah," said Struan. "All you ever do is run away from us every break-time."

"And shout at people," added Katya, fiddling with the bracelet around her wrist.

"JUST SHUT UP AND PUT HIM BACK," I shouted.

"Keep your hair on," muttered Joe, and he stopped dancing with Crow.

Then something awful happened. As Joe lifted Crow up into the air to put him back in his place, Crow's head fell off. Then Joe stood on it by mistake and left a big muddy footprint right over Crow's face.

Straight away, everyone stopped laughing and went quiet. They looked worried.

I glared at them all. And I reached for the worst word I knew. "You *idiots*."

I turned away from them all and walked off.

A few seconds later, the playground was silent. Everyone had gone inside even though the bell hadn't rung. I was all alone with Crow.

"Great job, Crow," I muttered as I put his head back on his neck. His eyes weren't shiny any more. "You're meant to scare them," I growled, "not have fun."

I was so cross I didn't see the thick grey storm clouds filling the sky.

CHAPTER 8

THE STORM

The storm hit the village at bath-time and got worse as I brushed my teeth. Dad was at his restaurant and Oliver was in charge of making sure I got to bed on time.

For a moment, we listened to the sound of the heavy rain outside.

"Night-night," Oliver said. "Funny things can happen in a storm but don't be scared of the thunder!" Then he went downstairs.

I closed my eyes and the sound of Sid squeaking softly soon made me feel sleepy. Just before I fell asleep, though, I remembered what Oliver had said about funny things happening in a storm. *Was my scarecrow going to be safe? What if something happened to him?*

Then I laughed at myself.

I wasn't laughing a few hours later, I can tell you that now.

*

In my dreams, I heard weird sounds.

BANG, SCRATCH, THUD. They got louder and louder. Suddenly I was awake. Those sounds were coming from downstairs, not my dreams.

My alarm clock said it was four in the morning. Sid gave a squeak.

The hall light came on. There was that noise again, as if something was banging on the front door.

"Whoever this is," Dad muttered, stomping past my room in his dressing-gown, "had better have a very good reason for waking me up."

A few moments later, he shouted up the stairs, "Kids? Can you come down a moment, please?"

I got up and padded down. So did Oliver. There was a smell of damp leaves in our house. I knew that smell but where was it from?

"Can either of you explain this?" said Dad.

Leaning outside the front door, dripping wet, was Crow.

CHAPTER 9

ALIVE

"How – how did he get here?" I stammered.

"Who was knocking on the door, Dad?" said Oliver.

And then the oddest thing happened. The little black mouth I'd drawn on Crow's face opened.

"*I* knocked on the door," said Crow. "With my broom handle."

"*What?*" we all said.

"I hopped all the way here," said Crow.

His pillow head tilted down a bit and looked at the stump of the old gate post. "On this."

"Incredible," I stammered.

"Not at all," said Crow. "It was easy. I went over the playground, up a field, past a well-dressed gentleman in a lovely waistcoat, then a sharp left ..."

"No," I said. "What's incredible is that you're *alive*."

"And can talk," said Dad softly.

He peered closer at Crow.

"Hey, that's *my* catering college T-shirt," Dad said, looking a bit upset. "*And* my jeans."

"And my cap," added Oliver.

"Sorry," I said. "I made do with what we had. It's my scarecrow. I made him."

"Never mind my jeans. More importantly – HOW IS IT EVEN ALIVE?" said Dad. "And ... I'm sorry, what did you say your name was?"

"Crow," said Crow.

"Right. Crow. Now listen. You're a very lovely scarecrow. However, it is late and I'm finding this all very weird. So why don't we all just go back to bed? Then we'll wake up in the morning and this will all have been just a dream," Dad said.

"But I am here to protect your daughter from mishap, misfortune and anyone who dares harm her," said Crow.

"Too many long words for the middle of the night," muttered Dad as he rubbed his eyes.

I sighed. "No, Crow. You're not meant to protect *me*. I built you to protect my den."

"The den? You mean the tree back at the school?" He frowned. "I'm there to protect *that*?"

"Yes. You're meant to stand there and frighten children away from the den."

"Oh," said Crow. "The children? The ones who danced with me?" He gave a little laugh. "I liked the dancing." He gave a little hop and hummed a tune.

"I didn't make you to dance. I made you to scare away the children," I said.

Crow looked down at the ground, then back at me. "Why?" he asked.

"That den belongs to me," I explained.

Crow blinked. "Doesn't it belong to—"

"Off you go," I said quickly. "You're letting all the cold air in."

"Bye, Crow," said Dad, shutting the door.

A few seconds later we heard a faint tapping sound as Crow hopped off – on his way back to school, with any luck.

Dad squinted at me. "Did that really happen?"

"Yup."

"Hattie," Oliver said softly as we went up the stairs. "That. Was. Amazing."

I grinned. It *was* kind of amazing. Even though I hadn't quite planned it, Crow coming to life was amazing.

But back in my room, I began to worry. Would Crow go back to normal after the storm ended? I didn't really know what to do with a living scarecrow.

CHAPTER 10

BOOOOO

At break-time the next day, I ran to the den to see Crow.

He was totally still – nothing moved.

It was just the storm then, I thought, with a mixture of relief and sadness. Maybe it was just as well.

Then Crow tipped his head to one side.

"Hello, maker," he said. "May I say how lovely it was to meet your family last night?"

"You can just call me Hattie," I gasped.

Suddenly, there was the sound of footsteps. Crow went still.

"I see *that* thing keeps turning up," Struan said, looking at Crow. "Like a bad pony."

"Penny," said Katya, with a grin at me.

Once again, we both nearly laughed together at what Struan had said. But I didn't want to forget what I'd made Crow for. I couldn't forget my squished hedgehogs. Or my den.

"*Now*," I said to Crow. "Go on. Be scary."

Crow's pillowcase face slowly turned towards Struan and Katya. They gasped.

"Welcome to the den," he said slowly. "I enjoyed dancing with you yesterday."

"*No*," I hissed. "Crow, you're here to frighten them *away*."

"*Not* welcome to the den," said Crow, waggling about on his fence-post stump. "Not one bit. Ignore what I just said."

"Is ... is it ...?" stammered Struan.

"Is it talking?" said Katya.

"I am," said Crow. "Clever girl. Do you like the mouth I have? It was drawn on."

"More scary," I whispered. "Make your eyes cross."

"BOOOOO," said Crow, waggling his broom-handle arms.

Struan and Katya held on tight to each other and then ran back across the playground, screaming. I'd had my doubts about Crow for a minute but this result was better than I'd dreamed of.

"Great job," I said, patting Crow on his broom-handle back. And this time I meant it. "That was perfect. Well, almost. We need to work out what you're going to say but ..."

The mouth I had drawn on Crow stretched until he grinned from one end of the pillow to the other.

"You thought I did a good job?" said Crow. His black Sharpie eyes were a bit blurry.

He gave two tiny watery blinks. He opened his mouth to say something, swallowed, then said, "*You* are welcome."

"Now stay here and do exactly the same to anyone else who tries to come into the den and mess things up."

"What will you do?" he asked.

"I will be alone," I said. "Making things without worrying that someone will tread on them or mess them up or squish them ..."

And that's *exactly* what I did. I mended my hedgehogs. I made a daisy chain. I sat on the floor of the den and looked up at the leaves and smiled.

Sometimes I'd hear footsteps outside the den but Crow would lift his arms and say "Booooo", and then there would be gasps and screams and whoever was outside would run away. The den was safe. It was all mine. My plan was working perfectly.

When the bell rang, I got up with a big grin on my face.

"I was scary?" said Crow proudly. "I protected you?"

"Um, sure."

At that point, I should have stopped and told him again that he was meant to protect the den, not me. That was my first mistake. But I was too excited to think about it just then.

"Keep it up!" I added.

That was my second mistake. I should not have said keep it up.

CHAPTER 11

NOT A BAD IDEA

Later that day we had a cooking class. As we trooped into the small cookery room, Mrs Simmonds pointed to the bags of flour and sugar on the table in front of us.

"We're going to bake for our village party. Little Plug is going to be 300 years old next weekend, and we're going to have a fair on the green to celebrate," she said.

"And our class has been chosen *specially* to make the cakes. We're going to sell them to raise money for a new playground on the village green. Isn't that wonderful? We'll do a practice bake today."

Mrs Simmonds split us into small groups to find a recipe and plan our cakes. Everyone but me wanted to make a carrot cake.

"It's going to sell like hot snakes," said Struan happily.

"Hot *cakes*, Struan," mumbled Katya, but this time she didn't look over at me or grin.

"Can't we make chocolate cake?" I mumbled. I didn't like carrots. But everyone ignored me. Or maybe they just didn't hear me. I started to feel in a bad mood.

I glared out of the window towards the den and for a tiny second Crow saw me looking at him. He saw that I was fed up.

Someone passed me some eggs to crack. A few minutes passed.

And that was when we heard it. A strange tapping noise from outside the cookery room. It was the sound of an old wooden fence post hopping on linoleum ...

All of a sudden, there he was.

"None of you are welcome," said Crow. He lifted his arms and then waggled back and forth on his pole. It was spooky.

Someone began to cry. Mrs Simmonds dropped a box of eggs on the floor.

"Apart from my maker," grinned Crow, his black smile stretching back into a big smile. "*You* are welcome. The rest of you ..." and he glared at everyone else, "are not welcome in the den. BOOOOO!"

Everyone screamed, including Mrs Simmonds.

"Wh-what are you?" she gasped.

"I am SCARY," said Crow.

"I can see that," Mrs Simmonds murmured. "But why are you here?"

"To protect *her*," Crow said, pointing at me.

I groaned. "No, Crow, you're meant to protect the ..."

But then I stopped. Every single child in the classroom was looking at me. Just like they'd looked at me that first awful lunch-time. This time they were frightened of me.

No one was laughing at me now.

I felt all sorts of different things. Pride at what I'd made. Anger that he hadn't stayed where I'd told him to. Worry it was all getting a tiny bit out of hand. But mostly I felt excited. Crow would do anything for me. Perhaps this could work out well?

"Hattie?" Mrs Simmonds said. "How is this scarecrow moving and talking?"

"Um ..." The words got mixed up as I tried to answer. "I ..."

"She can do everything," said Crow softly, looking at me. "She is my maker."

Mrs Simmonds took a deep breath and looked at the ceiling. When she looked back down again, she said in a calm voice, "Well, Hattie, your friend is going to have to wait outside until the end of the school day. We need to get on with making these cakes. Off you go, scarecrow."

Crow gave her a terrible scowl. He was getting more and more scary by the second. What had happened to the rather sweet, damp, messy thing that turned up at our cottage last night?

Mrs Simmonds turned to our class. "Now, if we can all check that our ovens have preheated ..."

My group began to grate the carrots for our carrot cake. I looked over at Crow. I hate carrot cake. Crow suddenly opened his mouth and said, "BOOOOOOO!"

It was the loudest boo he had made yet. And the longest.

And then he hopped all the way across the classroom until he was next to me.

"What do you think you are doing?" Mrs Simmonds cried. "WHO SAID YOU COULD JOIN MY CLASS?"

But every time she spoke, Crow would shout out "BOO!" and waggle his broom-handle arms about.

I knew what he was doing.

He was *protecting me.*

The other children were looking over at me as if they wanted me to make him stop.

"Can I be of any more assistance?" Crow asked me once Mrs Simmonds had stopped talking.

"Well, seeing as you're here," I said after a moment, "no one on this table wanted to make chocolate cake. But that's my favourite."

There was a splintering sound as Crow bent his broom handle. He put both ends on the table, leaned over and looked at everyone in turn.

"Make whatever type of cake she wants," he growled in a low voice.

And everyone nodded. Struan slowly scraped the grated carrot into the bin.

I looked at Crow happily. *Thank you,*
I thought, *you're the best idea I've ever had.*

CHAPTER 12

GETTING MORE FRIGHTENING

The next week went even better – well, the first half at least. Crow protected me from having to queue for lunch and tidy up after Art.

And when I didn't want to wear my scratchy school jumper and started wearing my favourite soft hoody instead, Crow protected me from getting into trouble about that as well.

Every time a teacher asked me to do something I didn't want to do, I'd give Crow a nod. Then he would glare at them with his scary eyes and say "BOOOOO!" It was like a battle and he would always win.

Sometimes he would hop up and down on his fence post too. That was when you knew he was really mad. There was something about the way he scowled that made everyone terrified.

It was impressive. And scary. Even I was getting scared. And Crow never left my side. If anyone asked him to, he'd tell them they were not welcome over and over until in the end they would just go. Everyone in my class avoided me. In fact, everyone at school avoided me.

As for the den? Thanks to Crow, I had the den to myself every lunch break. And morning break. And afternoon break. Every break, in fact.

It was quiet in there. Very quiet. And it turns out there's only so many mud hedgehogs a girl can make.

Sometimes, I'd hear the sounds of my classmates playing in the playground and for one tiny split second, I'd think about what they were doing and if it was any fun.

Once, I even stuck my head out of the den because I could hear children laughing at something and I wanted to see what. But Crow turned his head and gave me the most scary glares of all his glares so far.

I gasped.

"Crow," I said in a shaky voice. "You're not meant to frighten *me*."

"I'm sorry," Crow said sadly. "I can't help it any more."

"Can't help *what*?" I said.

"I am getting more and more terrifying," he said in a terrifying way. "My *terrifying* skills are growing like corn in the sun."

"I didn't think of that when I made you," I admitted.

"You weren't to know," he said sadly.

For a second, we were silent. A black bird darted past us in the sky. It made a funny crow cry.

The effect on Crow was instant. His head snapped to the left. His broom-handle arms waggled and jerked. He looked at the crow as if he wanted to fly away too.

When the crow was gone, Crow gave a long sigh.

"Are you all right, Crow?" I said.

"BOOOOOOOOOOOOOOOOOOOOO," said Crow, and for a second it sounded like he was crying. Then he shouted, "Now get back in your den and STAY THERE!"

"You're not meant to shout at me," I muttered, but I did as he asked.

"You built me to frighten children," said Crow, "and, sadly, that is all I can now do. Before too long, I will be frightening myself."

He was unhappy. I was unhappy.

Oh, Hattie, what have you done?

CHAPTER 13

THINGS HAVE TO CHANGE

The next morning, a Saturday, was bright and sunny. It was the day of the village party. Villagers started bringing tables and bunting, chairs and stalls. We were all busy making the village green look nice and ready for the village fair.

There was a cake stall with our chocolate cake right in the middle, a brass band, some vegetable displays, and stalls selling home-made jam. It would have been lovely, except for one thing.

Crow.

Right now, he was standing near the cake stall, with his broom-handle arms folded, staring grimly at me and everyone else. He looked like he was guarding the cake. Perhaps he'd shout at anyone who tried to eat it – I didn't know what he might do. When he wasn't glaring at kids and grown-ups, he would sometimes look up at the crows darting across the sky and sigh a big sigh.

I tried my hardest to look and act normal, but having Crow around now made me feel as if I had something heavy sitting on my chest. He protected me *too* much. I couldn't talk to anyone or look at anyone without him starting a fight. I'd had enough, but I didn't know how to get rid of him.

As the village green got more crowded, I tried to get away from him. His stare was one million times worse than my scratchy school jumper. I couldn't remember the last time I'd been alone, apart from in my bed. I couldn't remember, when it came to it, the last time I'd smiled or chatted to anyone except Oliver or Dad.

I went and stood next to a craft table. Laid out on a pretty red-and-white tablecloth was a collection of pottery and pincushions and bead bracelets. They were beautiful and I felt as if I had seen them before.

I bent down and picked up the label of the nearest bracelet.

"MADE BY KATYA," it read.

I stared at it.

Katya?

Suddenly, I remembered that every time I made something at school, Katya had admired it. I thought she'd been laughing at me.

The way she'd reached out to my leaves ... The way she'd looked at my food face ... That first lunch-time, when she'd asked if I'd wanted to play and I had thought she was talking to everyone but me.

Perhaps ...

Perhaps I'd got things all wrong?

I spun around and found myself looking right at Katya.

"Did you really make all of these?" I asked.

Her green eyes peered into mine. For a second, I thought she was about to walk away from me as quickly as she could. Why wouldn't she? Ever since I'd arrived at school, either I or Crow had shouted at her and tried to scare her away from the den – and it was all my fault.

But Katya gave me a warm smile. "Yeah."

"You like making things too?" I said.

She nodded. "I'm always making things. When you came to our school and I saw the things you made ... well, I'd hoped we might be—"

Whatever she was about to say, she had to stop. We heard the hopping and booing sounds we knew so well.

Coming through the crowds was my scarecrow, with a face like thunder, his broom-handle arms waggling and spinning fast. He knocked a cup of tea out of an old lady's hand and when she said "Excuse me!" he snarled back at her "Deal with it, granny."

Then he pogo-ed over to where me and Katya were standing.

"Is she giving you trouble?" Crow hissed from his big black mouth, which seemed to have grown bigger than the last time I'd looked at it.

He didn't wait for my reply. He spun round to face Katya and began a huge, terrifying BOOOOOO!

I saw her step back. I looked around me and saw the villagers all stare together at this monster I had made.

I knew that if Crow scared Katya away from me one more time, she and I would never be friends. I knew now that if Crow kept everyone away from me, I would always be alone.

Something had to change. I had made him to protect a den, but I was never going to have any friends if Crow went on scaring children away from me.

At last, I said, "Stop this, Crow."

Crow put his arms down and turned around. He looked surprised and even a bit pleased.

That nasty frown became a bit less fierce.

"Stop?" he asked hopefully.

"Yes," I said. "You can stop now."

"Stop scaring people for you?" he said in a very soft voice.

"Yes. Please," I told him.

"Did I – do a good job?" he asked. Suddenly he sounded as if he needed someone to help him.

"You were amazing, Crow," I said. "But things went wrong. I should never have wanted the den all to myself. I shouldn't have made you protect me."

I should have just shared the den. I'd done everything wrong. But perhaps I could make things better – for him. And for me.

The brass band was warming up. We could hear them on the other side of the village green. I spotted Joe and Struan. They were looking at Crow with worried faces.

Suddenly, I remembered something that had happened when I first made Crow. "Crow," I said, "would you like to dance? Like you did before?"

He gave me a big smile. His eyes went wide. "Yes," he said. "Very much."

CHAPTER 14

THE FIELD

The rest of the day was so much fun. Crow
danced all afternoon with almost everyone
in the village, while I ate cake, jumped on the
bouncy castle till I felt sick, and ran around the
village green with my new friends.

"So do you think you're going to enjoy living
in Little Plug now?" asked Katya as the sun
began to set and the sky filled with pink and
orange.

"Yeah," I said. "I like it actually. Will
you – will you show me how you made those
bracelets?"

"Yes, if you show me how you made the leaves with the dandelions," said Katya.

"Deal," I said.

We grinned. Crow was dancing a jig with Oliver. Crow was still smiling but he looked as if he needed a rest. He was dancing slower and slower.

"What are you going to do with Crow?" Katya asked. "Now you don't need him to guard the tree any more?"

"What he really needs is somewhere lovely to stand outside, with a friend to keep him company ..." I said.

I gasped, then laughed aloud. "Katya, are you good at sewing? There's something we have to make."

*

A while later, Crow and I were walking up a field, together with Dad, Oliver, Katya and Struan.

"Do you think you'll be happy here, Crow?" I said. "Look, there's lots of crows to scare. And you can see over the whole village. And there's a friend here already." I pointed to the other scarecrow that Dad and I had seen before.

"He has such beautiful clothes," gasped Crow. "I'd feel shabby next to him."

"We can help with that," said Katya.

From my bag I pulled out a beautiful red velvet waistcoat. "We made this for you."

Crow's mouth made an O of surprise, then two little ink blots fell down his cheek.

"You made that for *me*?" he gasped. "My own waistcoat?" I could tell he really liked it.

"Fit for a king," said Struan wisely. Katya and I looked at him, surprised. Struan had, for once, said the right thing.

We walked over to the middle of the field and found the right spot for Crow. Then I lifted him high in the air and let his fence post go deep into the soil. I put the waistcoat over his T-shirt.

"If you look over there," I whispered to Crow, "you can see the playground of Little Plug Primary School, so I won't be far away."

"You just give me a shout if anyone gives you any trouble," said Crow, and he gave me a wink.

"I will," I said with a smile.

Then I patted him one last time. "Bye, Crow." I looked him in the eyes. "You are a good scarecrow."

"Booo," he whispered.

"Booo," I said back.

Then he gave a big yawn. "I am sleepy."

I said, "When you wake up, you will have lots of crows to scare."

Just before his eyes closed, he smiled.

I stood very still for a bit and thought about what had happened. I looked at Crow's face and felt sad and happy all at once.

Then I walked back to the others.

By the time we got to the bottom of the field, Crow was standing totally still, with the last rays of the golden sunset shining all around him.

I lifted my hand and waved goodbye to him.

And then we all went home for tea.

Our books are tested
for children and young people by
children and young people.

Thanks to everyone who consulted on
a manuscript for their time and effort in
helping us to make our books better
for our readers.